Santa Claus

CHEX BOOKS NEW YORK

It was Christmas Eve. At the North Pole, where Santa Claus lives, everyone was very busy. For weeks the elves had been hard at work. They had made and wrapped up hundreds of presents for Santa to deliver. There were presents everywhere, of all shapes and sizes. Each was wrapped in bright paper. It was a wonderful sight.

Outside, Santa's sleigh was
almost ready for his journey
around the world.
The elves had given it a new
coat of paint and it shone
in the winter sunshine.
In the stables were six fine
reindeer. They had all had their
coats washed and brushed. Even
their antlers had been polished,
ready for their great ride
through the night.

At last it was time to load the presents onto the sleigh. The elves worked hard all afternoon until the sleigh was piled high. It was so full of presents that there was barely enough room for Santa to sit! The reindeer were brought out and one by one they were tied to the front of the sleigh. The bells on their bridles jingled merrily.

Finally Santa Claus arrived.
He was dressed in red.
"Well done, my friends!" he said.
"Everything looks splendid!"
He patted each of the reindeer.
Then he sprinkled them with magic
dust so that they could fly.
"Away we go!" he cried.
The sleigh began to rise slowly
into the dark night air.

They hadn't gone far when it
began to snow. The snow got thicker
and thicker. Soon they could
hardly see where they were going.
"That looks like a rooftop down
there!" cried Santa, peering
through the swirling snow.
The reindeer flew downward
and landed with a bump. They
hadn't landed on a rooftop. They
had landed in a huge snowdrift!

"That's not a very good start,"
said Santa as he brushed the snow
from his jacket. "We'll have to
be more careful!"
He picked up some presents that
had fallen out of the sleigh.
They set off once more. It was
still snowing very hard.
Finally, Santa had to admit
they were lost.
"We'll never deliver these
presents on time," he sighed.

They saw a wise old owl sitting in a tree. The owl blinked in surprise when he saw the sleigh, but he was able to tell Santa the way to the nearest town. "At last!" cried Santa as the rows of rooftops came into view. "Now we can make a start!" The reindeer landed softly on the first rooftop and Santa climbed down the chimney with his sack of presents.

He landed in the fireplace
and then wished he hadn't.
Someone had left a bunch of holly
there. He jumped up with it
sticking to his bottom.
"I wish people would be more
careful," he said, pulling
the holly out. "It would be so much
easier if I could come through
the front door like everyone else!"

Santa worked all through the
night, going up and down
chimneys of all shapes and sizes.
Once he got stuck. When he came
out at the bottom, his clothes were
covered with soot.
''They were clean this morning,''
he sighed.
In another house he nearly burned
his beard when he found the ashes
of a fire still hot.

"Some people do make my job
difficult," he said. "Still, there aren't
many more houses to go!"
He came to the very last house.
There he found some cake and
a glass of milk waiting for him.
"How nice," he said. "Just what
I need before I go home!"
He sat down in a chair and
started to eat the cake.

The house was warm and Santa was
very tired. It wasn't long before
he was fast asleep.
Up on the roof the reindeer began
to get worried. Santa had been
gone a long time and soon it
would start to get light.
They peered through the windows
and tapped on the glass until
Santa woke up.
"Thank you, my friends," he said.
"I must have fallen asleep!"

He climbed into the sleigh and they set off for home. Without the presents on board the sleigh was much lighter. They headed quickly back toward the snowy lands of the north.

They arrived safely home just as dawn was breaking.

"Well done, all of you," said Santa. He led the reindeer back to the stables. "I think we all need some sleep!"

Santa awoke later that morning feeling much better.
He remembered it was Christmas Day. He smiled as he thought of everyone waking up all over the world and opening their presents. He looked at the foot of his bed and saw a stocking filled with presents for himself.
"Well, imagine that," he said.
"Who could have given me these? Merry Christmas, everyone!"

Say these words again

Santa Claus	careful
wrapped	elves
paint	cake
shapes	milk
ride	soot
beard	tapped
swirling	climbed